THE RAINS ARE COMING

by Sanna Stanley

Greenwillow Books New York

The artwork was reproduced from etchings
with aquatints.
The text type is Weidemann Book.

Library of Congress Cataloging-in-Publication Data
Stanley, Sanna.
   The rains are coming / by Sanna Stanley.
       p.   cm.
   Summary: As Aimee, the daughter of a missionary
in Zaire, gathers her friends for a party, the
sky grows more and more threatening.
   ISBN 0-688-10948-9. ISBN 0-688-10949-7 (lib. bdg.)
   [1. Zaire—Fiction.   2. Rain and rainfall—Fiction.]
I. Title.   PZ7.S7895Rai   1993
[E]—dc20   92-1347   CIP   AC

Aimee's family had been living in Zaire for four months, and all that time the sky had been gray. Every day Aimee thought it might rain, but it never did.

"Now is it time for my party?"
Aimee asked, as she and her
mother were setting the picnic
table.
"As soon as your father gets here,"
said her mother.
Aimee's father was a missionary.
He traveled to nearby villages
where he trained people to be
pastors and teachers.
"Run along and get your friends,"
said Aimee's mother. "He'll be
here soon."

Aimee found Luzolo pounding
manioc into flour. "It's time for
my party, Luzolo," she called.
Luzolo and all her Zairian friends
spoke both French and their own
language, Kikongo. Aimee had
learned French in Belgium before
coming here. Now she was
learning Kikongo.
"I'll be there soon, Aimee," said
Luzolo. She looked at the small
clouds moving across the sky.
"Have to hurry," she said.
"*Zimvula zeti kwiza.*"

Siamu and her father were mending a fish trap.

"Siamu, it's time for my party," said Aimee.

"I'll be there soon," said Siamu. Siamu's father glanced up at the sky. Thick clouds were rising.

"Have to hurry," he said.

"*Zimvula zeti kwiza*," added Siamu.

"Hand me that thatch, please,"
Matondo called down from
the roof.
"It's time for my party," Aimee
announced.
Matondo pointed up. "I'll be
there soon," she said.
The sky had turned a heavy
gray.
"Have to hurry," she said.
"*Zimvula zeti kwiza.*"

Kiese had just come back from
the fields.
"It's time for my party, Kiese,"
said Aimee.
Kiese's mother looked up.
There was an orange glow in
the sky.
"You better hurry, girls," she
said. "*Zimvula zeti kwiza.*"

Aimee and Kiese ran into the
yard followed by Matondo.
"Grab that tablecloth," cried
Aimee's mother, as a gust of
wind rushed by.

Siamu and Luzolo ran into
the yard.
"Help me get the animals in
the shed," called Aimee.

Aimee's father drove up. Lightning flashed.
"It's time for my party, Dad," Aimee called. Thunder cracked. "Hurry!" she cried. *"Zimvula zeti kwiza!"*
Just in time, everyone moved inside.

And outside
it began to rain.

Author's Note

The Rains Are Coming is set in the lower western area of the Republic of Zaire, a large country in central western Africa. This area is slightly below the equator, and it has two major seasons a year: a rainy season when it is hottest, and a dry season when it is coldest.

Zimvula zeti kwiza means "the rains are coming" in Kikongo, one of the languages spoken in Zaire. (French is the official language.)

Manioc is a white, potato-like root. It is peeled and soaked in water before it is left out to dry in the sun. After it is dried, the manioc is pounded into flour, which the Zairians use to make many different foods.